CONTENTS

THE ANT AND THE GRASSHOPPER

It was a beautiful summer day in the cornfield. The sun was shining, and the sky was blue.

The Grasshopper was hopping about on his long legs playing tag with the butterflies. This is a day for singing, thought the Grasshopper.

"Chirrr-up! Chirrr-up! Chirrr-up!"

Just at that moment the Grasshopper came upon a large stone. It was nestled in the ground. It lay beneath the husk of a large ear of corn on a cornstalk.

TALES OF AESOP

RETOLD TIMELESS CLASSICS

Perfection Learning®

Retold by Karen Berg Douglas

Editor: Paula J. Reece
Designer: Jan M. Michalson
Illustrator: Sue F. Cornelison

For information, contact:
Perfection Learning® Corporation
1000 North Second Avenue, P.O. Box 500
Logan, Iowa 51546-0500.
Phone: 1-800-831-4190 • Fax: 1-712-644-2392

Paperback ISBN 0-7891-2845-4
Cover Craft® ISBN 0-7807-9006-5
Printed in the U.S.A.

"All that hopping and singing has made me rather tired," the Grasshopper said. "This is a nice shady place. I think I will rest a while."

So he sat down.

Just then a small black Ant passed by. He was carrying a big yellow kernel of corn on his back.

"Where are you going with that, my dear friend?" asked the Grasshopper.

"I am taking it to my nest," said the Ant. He huffed and puffed as he plodded along.

"You look very tired," said the Grasshopper. "Why don't you stop and take a little rest? Come and talk with me for a while. It's such a beautiful day. And the warm sun will feel so good on your back."

The Ant stopped and looked around. His back was sore, very sore. And he really wanted to. But he shook his head.

"No, I would really like to sit and talk with you, Mister Grasshopper," he replied. "But I am just too busy today."

" 'Too busy'? What do you mean?" chirped the Grasshopper.

"Well, I must get this corn to my nest so we have something to eat this winter," said the Ant.

"It won't be long before the ground gets hard and the snow begins to fly. Then it won't be so easy to find food."

"Nonsense, my dear friend," replied the Grasshopper. "Just look around. There is a lot of food to be found."

But the Ant just shook his head. He picked up the kernel of corn and went on his way.

One month passed. Then two.

And it wasn't long before the cold, wet winds of winter began to blow over the cornfield.

One morning the Grasshopper poked his head out of his warm nest in the ground. It was very quiet. There was no one around.

All the animals in the forest had settled down for the long, cold winter. So had the birds. And even the bugs.

The Grasshopper stretched his neck and peered at the sky.

The clouds were as white as the snow on the ground.

The Grasshopper shook his head. He could not remember when he had eaten his last meal. But he was so hungry.

He crawled back into his little nest.

"Oh, whatever will I do?" he said to himself. "Wherever will I find enough food for my dinner? I am so hungry."

The Grasshopper was very sad. He started to cry.

And that's when he saw them.

The little black Ants were scurrying back and forth on their thin, little black legs. They looked very happy. They were sharing the corn and grain that they had collected during the summer.

At that moment an old black Ant came by. He saw the sad look on the face of the Grasshopper.

"You must be hungry," he said. "And your nose is turning blue. Please, come and eat with us. We have enough for everyone."

"Me? You want me to join you?" the Grasshopper asked.

The old black Ant nodded yes.

"Thank you. Thank you so much. You are very kind, and I am very grateful," the Grasshopper chirped. And he began to follow the Ant.

"You are most welcome, my friend. But I hope you have learned a lesson," said the old black Ant. "You did not work last summer because you were too busy singing and hopping around."

"Yes, that is true. And I know now that I was wrong," said the Grasshopper. "I have learned that all of us must plan for tomorrow. So next summer things will be different.

"Next summer we will work hard together."

- *It is wise to prepare today for the needs of tomorrow.*

BELLING THE CAT

Mice have always had one big enemy.
The Cat.
Big cats. Small cats. Striped cats. Black cats.
Even playful kittens.
So this should come as no surprise. The mice have been plotting for many years on how to outwit cats.

Early one morning a long time ago, the mice called a general council meeting. It was to talk about their number one enemy.

"We must find a way to be safe from the Cat," said Old Gray Mouse with the long, long tail. He was leading the meeting.

"Yes, yes," they all agreed.

Then some said one thing and some said another. But as it turned out, no one could think of a good plan.

Finally after listening to all the arguments, Young Mouse stood up.

"My fellow mice, I have a good idea to share," he began.

"What is it? What is it?" everyone began to squeak.

"Well, as you all know, the Cat is very sly and sneaky," said Young Mouse. "If we knew when she was around, or when she was coming, we could get away from her quickly."

"That sounds sensible," said one of the older mice.

"You're right," said another.

"Good idea," squeaked a third.

Young Mouse beamed with pride.

"Then it's unanimous," said Old Gray Mouse. "This is our number one problem. Now, what do we do about it?"

"Well, I would like to propose that a small bell be tied to a ribbon. And the ribbon be placed around the neck of the Cat," said Young Mouse.

"Then we can hear her coming and going. We will always know when she's around."

"Great idea," said one of the older mice.

"Super idea," said another.

"Right on!" said a third.

Every mouse in the house squeaked its approval and shook its tail. Once again Young Mouse beamed with pride.

Finally Old Gray Mouse stood up again.

"I have listened with great interest to all the discussion," he said. "It is a wonderful idea. And no doubt it would be successful. But I have one question to ask."

Every mouse perked up a pink ear.

"Why, sure," said Young Mouse. "I'm sure I can find an answer for you very easily."

"All right then. Which one of you, my dear friends, will be willing to place the bell around the Cat's neck?" asked Old Gray Mouse.

Every mouse looked at the other.

But no one squeaked out a word.

- It is easy to propose a suggestion, but sometimes it is difficult to carry out the remedy.

THE GOOSE WITH THE GOLDEN EGGS

Once upon a time there lived a Farmer who had a big, white goose with a bright orange beak.

It was a good goose.

Every morning the Farmer would get up from his bed. Next he would set the table for breakfast and walk to the barn.

And every morning he would find a big, white egg. He would carry it back to his house to cook for his breakfast.

"You are such a fine goose," the Farmer would say as he reached into her nest to take the egg. "I know I am very lucky to have you."

Now this went on for many years. And the Farmer was very happy.

And so was the goose.

But one morning the Farmer went to the barn. And there was no big, white egg in the nest of the goose.

In its place was a bright yellow one that sparkled and glittered.

When the Farmer tried to pick it up, it was very heavy—as heavy as a bowling ball!

Why, what is this? he thought. Is someone trying to play a trick on me?

But the egg was so pretty that he decided to take it home. He wanted to show all his friends what his wonderful goose had given him.

So the Farmer went to his shed. He got out his wheelbarrow and very carefully placed the beautiful egg into it. Then he wheeled it into his house.

Once inside he saw that the egg was far more beautiful than any egg he had ever seen in his life!

But the Farmer got another surprise when he carried it to the window. Once the sun shone on it, the Farmer could see that the egg was made of pure GOLD!

"I can't believe this," said the Farmer. "Soon I will be the richest man in the village!"

And so he was.

Each morning the Farmer went to the barn and reached into the nest of the goose. And there was another golden egg.

Each afternoon he took the egg to the market and sold it.

Soon he was the richest man for many miles around.

But as the Farmer grew very rich, he also grew very greedy.

"This goose is giving me only one golden egg every day," he said. "If she would give me two, three, or even four, I could be even richer."

So the next morning when the Farmer went to the barn, he reached down into the nest again.

"What? Only one golden egg again?" he shouted.

The poor goose looked up at him with sad eyes.

"You must give me two golden eggs tomorrow morning. Or you will die!" shouted the Farmer in a very loud voice.

The big, white goose sat very still.

The next morning the Farmer went to the barn again. He reached into the nest. But there was only one golden egg.

The poor goose began to shake with fear.

"What did I tell you yesterday?" said the Farmer. "You had a warning, you silly goose."

And with that, he killed his beautiful white bird.

"Now I will get all of your golden eggs at once," he said.

The Farmer opened up the goose. But when he looked inside his once beautiful bird, he found nothing.

- Don't be too greedy. You may end up with nothing.

THE fOx
WiTHOUT a TaiL

Early one morning the Fox decided he would take a little walk in the forest.

He had not gone too far when he heard a snap!

He had caught his bushy tail in a trap!

"Oh, my, what should I do?" he cried.

He reached around and began to pull and tug. And tug and pull. And finally he yanked himself free.

But when the Fox turned around, his bushy tail was still in the trap!

Now a tail is very important to a fox. Especially if it's a big, brown, bushy one like his was.

And so he was very sad.

So for several days the Fox stayed inside his lair. He was ashamed to show his face to his fellow foxes. He feared they would laugh at him.

"For the rest of my life I will be the only fox in the whole wide world without a tail," he said sadly.

As soon as the Fox said the words out loud to himself, he thought of something. What if no fox had a tail? Then he would not be different.

So the next day the Fox held a meeting in the forest hall. He invited all of his fellow foxes to come.

Once they began to arrive, he stood in the shadows with his back to the wall. He did this so they could not see the spot where his tail once was.

When everyone was there, the Fox stepped forward and thanked them for coming. He told them he had an idea to share.

"What is it?" asked one.

"Yes, tell us," said another.

"Well, the other day I was thinking how each one of us could look much more fashionable. I think we should do away with our tails," the Fox said.

His friends were wide-eyed as they looked at one another. They then looked at the Fox with surprise.

"Are you saying we should cut off our tails?" asked one.

"Why not?" replied the Fox, with a sly smile. "Just think how much faster you could run without it. Especially if you're being chased by a man or a dog.

"And think about how difficult it is to sit down. It's always in the way. Even when you try to sit in a nice, soft chair," the Fox continued.

"In fact, we really don't use our tails for anything," the Fox said. "We may as well be rid of them. They are nothing but trouble to us."

His fellow foxes fell silent. No one said a word.

Then an old fox stepped forward.

"My dear friend Fox," he began. "It is all well and good for you to bring an idea to all of us. But before we reply, will you please turn around?"

The Fox turned red and stared at the ground.

"You see, my dear friend," said the old fox. "I do not think you have been honest with us.

"I do not think you would have told us to do this if you had not lost your own."

- Before you take any advice, be sure you will benefit from it.

THE HARE AND THE TORTOISE

Now some people may tell you that any animal can run much faster than a turtle or a tortoise.

That may be true—except for the Hare.

One morning many years ago, all the animals of the forest gathered under a tree for a party.

The Lion was there. So was the Tiger. And the Fox. Along with the Deer and the Woodchuck.

"I bet if we had a race, I could beat any one of you," said the Hare. "I am the fastest animal in the world."

"I'm too busy to play games today," said the Lion.

"Me too," said the Tiger.

"Me too," said the Fox.

"Count me out," said the Woodchuck. "I have to fix my house. The heavy rain last night nearly swept it away in the river."

"I would take you up on that race," said the Deer, who runs very swiftly. "But I promised to go walking in the woods today with my children."

"Aw, you're all too afraid because you know I will win," said the Hare.

"Don't be too sure of that," said a soft, little voice. "I'll be glad to race you for the honor."

"You? Who?" asked the Hare again.

"Me," replied the voice.

"Me who?" said the Hare.

"Look down here on the ground," said the voice.

All the animals looked down on the ground. There they saw a tiny brown tortoise. Everyone knows what a slowpoke a tortoise is.

"Is this a joke?" asked the Hare. "Do you know that I have never been beaten by any animal in the forest?"

"I have heard that said," replied the Tortoise.

"Well, then, my silly little friend, what makes you think you can beat me?" snorted the Hare. "It certainly isn't your size."

And with that, all the animals in the forest began to laugh.

"I am here to tell you that I accept your challenge," said the Tortoise.

"That is a good joke," said the Hare. "But I would be at the finish line before you took three steps."

Then the Hare began to laugh even more.

Now a Bluebird began to feel a little sorry for the Tortoise. He had been sitting in a tree watching all that was going on.

"Just a minute, Mr. Hare," the Bluebird chirped. "In the beginning you said that you bet you could beat 'anyone.' So why don't you give our little friend, the Tortoise, the chance he deserves?"

"You silly bird," said the Hare. "That would be a big waste of my time."

"But you said you could beat 'anyone,' " the Bluebird insisted. "And it's only fair that you give the Tortoise his chance."

"That's right," said the Lion.

"That's right," said the Fox.

And all the other animals agreed with them.

"Well, all right then," said the Hare. "But as far as I am concerned, this is no race at all. I don't even need a rabbit's foot in my pocket."

And everyone laughed again.

The next morning just before dawn, all the animals gathered at the side of the dirt road, just outside the forest. It was decided that they would race to the big oak tree. That was about three miles down the road.

The Lion drew a big line in the road. Meanwhile the Tortoise and the Hare rolled up their sleeves and got ready to run.

"I'll tell you when to start," said the Lion. He held up a big red and white flag. "All right. On your mark. Get ready. Get set. GO!"

The race was on.

The Hare took off as fast as his feet would carry him. When he got halfway down the road, he stopped and turned around. He wanted to see how far the Tortoise had gone.

"Oh, my, he's only moved a few steps," said the Hare. "I knew this would be an easy race to win."

In fact, the Hare thought it was so easy that he lay down under a tree. He thought he would take a little nap until the Tortoise caught up with him.

Meanwhile the tiny Tortoise plodded on and on.

All of a sudden, the Hare woke up and looked around. The Tortoise was nowhere in sight.

"Aha! I knew I could beat that silly tortoise," the Hare said.

And with that, he began to run as fast as he could toward the finish line. All the animals stood waiting.

"Where have you been?" asked the Lion.

"Oh, I'm sorry," said the Hare. "When I saw how slow the Tortoise was, I decided to take a little nap."

"That was a big mistake," said the Lion.

"Why, what do you mean?" asked the Hare. "Where is the Tortoise?"

"He's under the big green oak tree, taking his little nap," said the Lion. "You see, while you were sleeping, the Tortoise crossed the finish line."

"But that can't be," said the Hare.

"Well, it is," said all the animals together.

"It may have taken him a little longer than it would have taken you, but he stayed with it," said the Lion. "The Tortoise is the winner."

- It is better to be slow and careful than fast and careless.

THE LION, THE FOX AND THE BEASTS

Once upon a time, in the middle of a dark green forest, lived a lion who was very lazy.

In fact, he was so lazy that he never wanted to hunt like other lions did. He didn't like to go out in the woods and hunt for his own breakfast and dinner.

So it wasn't long before he became very sick from not eating.

"Oh, what shall I do? What shall I do? I am so hungry," he groaned one morning.

Yet all he did was lie there and complain.

"If I could only find an easy way to get something to eat. Maybe then I would get big and strong again," he muttered.

That was important to the Lion. After all, he was the King of the Forest.

That night as the Lion lay awake in his bed, he came up with a plan.

"I know what I can do. I will tell everyone that I am dying. And I want them to come and visit with me a while to hear my last words of wisdom," he said.

Then he chuckled and roared. And soon he fell asleep.

Early the next morning the Lion got up from his bed and lay down in the door of his den. He started to moan and groan.

Just then a Goat came by.

"Why, what is the matter with you today?" asked the Goat.

"Oh, I am so sick," said the Lion. "I am so sick that I think I will die."

"Oh, you poor thing," said the Goat. "Please, my dear friend, is there anything I can do for you during your last days on Earth?"

"Oh, yes," replied the Lion. "I am so lonely. It would mean so much if you would come in and visit with me for a while."

"I can do that. I know how it feels to be lonely," said the Goat. And he went into the

Lion's den with the Lion following close behind.

A few days later the Lion went to the door of his den again. Once again he lay down and began moaning and groaning.

"Why, what is the matter?" asked the Sheep.

He had been in the field. When he heard the Lion's cry, he quickly came running.

"Oh, I am so sick, Mister Sheep. I think I will die," said the Lion.

"Oh, my dear friend," said the Sheep. "Is there anything I can do for you?"

"Well, as a matter of fact, there is," said the Lion. "I am so lonely. I just feel like talking. Won't you come in and visit with me for a while?"

"Yes, yes, of course. I'd be glad to do that," said the Sheep. And in he went with the Lion following close behind.

A few days later a Calf heard the moaning and groaning of the Lion. He, too, decided he had better stop by and see what was happening.

The Lion was lying, once again, at the door to his den.

"Are you all right?" mooed the shy Calf.

"Well, not really," said the Lion. "I think I am dying. And I need to share my last thoughts with someone. Someone young like you."

"I would be glad to hear them," said the Calf. "But perhaps I should go and tell my mother where I am."

"Well, I'm sure it wouldn't matter to her if you only stayed a few minutes," said the Lion. "And it would mean so much to me."

The Calf thought a moment.

"You're right. My mother will not mind. And I have a lot of time," said the Calf, heading toward the Lion's lair. And in he went.

Now in case you're wondering, this was not too surprising.

After all, no one ever turns down a request from the King of the Forest. Not even a Rabbit, a Wild Turkey, or a Deer.

Like the other animals, they, too, stopped to visit with their sick friend for a while.

Several days later the clever Lion seemed to be feeling much better. He was smiling happily when he looked out his door and saw the Fox.

"My, you're looking well today," said the Fox.

"Oh, yes, but I have been so sick and so lonely, my dear friend Fox," said the Lion. "A few of my kind friends in the forest have come to visit me. But why not you, Mister Fox?"

"I have been very busy," said the Fox.

"Well, won't you come in and talk with me a while now?" asked the Lion.

The Fox looked at the old Lion with a sly smile. Then he shook his head no.

"And why not?" asked the Lion.

"I see by all the tracks around here that you have had many, many visitors during the past few weeks," the Fox said. "So you must not have been too lonely."

"Well, that is true," said the Lion, "but I really would like to talk just with you."

"No, my friend. I don't think that will be possible," said the Fox, who was just as clever as the Lion.

"You see, I have noticed the many tracks from the animals going into your den. But I see no tracks of the animals coming out," said the Fox.

"So until I do, I think I will stay outside and wait a while."

- *Watch and learn what happens to others.*

THE MAN, THE BOY, AND THE DONKEY

Many years ago in a little town not so far away from here, there lived a man, his son, and a donkey.

One morning the man turned to his son and said, "I don't know what to do with that donkey. He doesn't do much of anything anymore except lie around and eat hay. I think I will sell him."

"That is a good idea, Father," said the son. "Let's take him to market tomorrow. There must be someone who can use a donkey. We can probably sell him and make some money."

So the next morning, the man and the boy got up very early. They tied a rope around the donkey's neck and started down the road.

It was a beautiful morning. The sun was shining. Flowers were blooming in the fields. And the air smelled so fresh following the gentle rain from the night before.

Before long they met an old woman.

"Good morning," said the man.

"Good morning," said the boy.

"Good morning to both of you," said the old woman. "And where may you be going today?"

"Why, we're going to the market to sell our donkey," said the man.

"To market?" she asked. "Why, that's a long way. Why don't you let the young boy ride the donkey so he won't get tired?"

The man and the boy looked at each other.

That sounded like a good idea. So the man helped the boy get up on the donkey's back, and they went on their way.

A few miles down the road, they met three men. They were pushing a cart full of vegetables.

"Good morning," said the man.

"Good morning," said the boy.

"Good morning to both of you," said the three men. "And where may you be going today?"

"Why, we're going to the market to sell our donkey," said the man.

"To market?" asked one of the men. "Why, that's a long way. You, boy, your legs are young and strong. Why don't you walk and let your poor old father ride?"

The man and his son looked at each other.

That sounded like a good idea. So the boy got off. He helped his father onto the donkey's back, and they went on their way.

They hadn't gone very far when they passed two women who were going to the market to sell some eggs.

"Shame on that big, strong, lazy man. He's making his poor little boy walk while he rides," said one to the other.

The man looked at his young son. At first he didn't know what to do. But finally he bent down, picked up his son, and placed him on the donkey's back too.

They rode this way a few more miles until they were almost to town.

"Look! Look!" said a young man. He was pointing at the man and his son on the donkey.

"Can you believe that?" asked another.

The man asked the donkey to stop. Then he called out to the people.

"Why are you pointing at my son, me, and the donkey?" he asked. "Why are you looking at us that way?"

The young man shook his finger at them.

"You should be ashamed of yourself for making that poor donkey carry both of you," said the young man. "You are strong and healthy. And you should be able to walk yourself."

"You two look more fit to carry the donkey than he is to carry you," said another.

The man and the boy looked at each other. They got off the donkey and tried to think what they should do.

"I know, I know," said the man at last. "I have a good idea. You wait here."

With that, he went to the nearby woods. He chopped down a big branch from the tree. Then he carried it back to the spot where his son and the donkey were waiting.

"Lie down," he said to the donkey.

The donkey did as it was told. Then the man tied the donkey's four feet to the branch with a strong rope. Finally the man and the boy raised the branch to their shoulders. The donkey was upside down!

Then they continued on their way to the market.

Everyone came out of their houses. They shouted and laughed at the man and the boy carrying the donkey.

They had never seen anything so silly in their lives!

But this time, the man and the boy paid no attention to the people.

Meanwhile the donkey was very unhappy. He didn't like to be carried upside down. And he didn't like to be laughed at!

Just as they reached the bridge leading into the market, the donkey got one of his feet loose. And he kicked out at the boy.

As he did, the boy dropped his end of the branch. And the donkey flew into the air, over the bridge, and into the river!

Three of his feet were still tied to the branch. So before anyone could save him, he drowned.

The man and the boy looked at each other.

They didn't know what to do.

"That will teach you," said the old woman who had followed them. "You listened to too many people as you came down the road. And now your donkey is gone forever."

- *When you try to please everyone, you please none.*

THE MISER AND HIS GOLD

Once upon a time many years ago, there lived a man who loved his money. He loved it so much that he never spent a penny unless he had to.

The people who lived in his village called him The Miser. This was because he was so greedy for gold coins.

All he wanted to do was look at his money, count it, and hold it in his hands.

"I must be the richest man in the world," gloated The Miser.

One day, thinking that someone might try to steal his money, he decided to bury it at the base of a tree in his garden.

But the next morning, he missed his money so much that he returned to the spot. He dug it up and counted it all over again.

Then he buried it again.

This went on for many years. And The Miser was so pleased that he had found such a good way to keep his money safe.

That is, until one morning.

That morning The Miser was busy counting his money. So busy that he did not see the robber behind the tree who was watching him!

Once again The Miser kissed his gold coins. Then he placed them in the ground, covered them with dirt, and left the garden.

As soon as he was gone, the robber went to the spot and dug them up.

The following morning when The Miser returned to his garden, he found nothing there under the tree but an empty hole.

"Robbers! Robbers!" he cried. "I have been robbed!"

The Miser began to weep and wail loudly. All of his neighbors came running.

"What has happened?" asked one of them.

"Well, I was always afraid someone would take my money away from me. So I buried it under the tree in my garden," said The Miser. "And now it's gone! I have been robbed!"

"Did you ever take any out to spend?" asked another.

"No, no, it was not to spend," said The Miser. "I just wanted it there to look at."

"Well, then, nothing so terrible has really happened to you," said yet another neighbor. "Here, come look at the hole. It will do you just as much good."

- Money has no real value if it is not used.

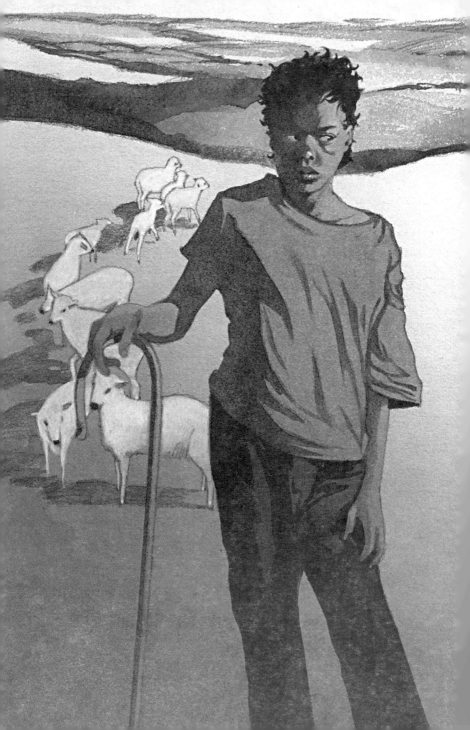

THE SHEPHERD BOY

Once upon a time in a small village at the base of some beautiful mountains, there lived a young Shepherd Boy.

Each morning he would get up before the sun came up. He would gather his flock of sheep around him and walk them up the hilly mountain to a fresh plot of green grass.

There they would graze and eat until they were happy and no longer hungry.

The Shepherd Boy loved his flock. They were like his children. He greeted each one by name every morning.

Sometimes he even talked to them as they climbed the hill.

"Come on, Lily Lamb, you're getting behind," he would say. And he would gently poke one of the slow sheep with his staff.

Or if one ran ahead, he would say, "Lena, slow down. Your brother can't keep up with you."

The sheep always listened to the Shepherd Boy. And they always did as they were told. They knew he would always take care of them and keep them safe.

Each time they reached the top of a hill, the Shepherd Boy would stop and count all of his sheep. Just to make sure each one was there before turning them loose.

"All right, go and eat now," he would say.

Then the Shepherd Boy would find a cool place under a shady tree. He would sit and wait there until they were through eating.

Sometimes while he waited, the Shepherd Boy sang to his sheep. Sometimes he closed his eyes and took a nap.

But most of the time he just sat and waited.

One day the Shepherd Boy became very lonely.

"I wish I had someone to talk to," he said sadly. "It is too quiet up here."

That night he thought of a plan.

The next morning he led his flock to the top of a hill once again. After he counted them and made sure each one was safe, the Shepherd Boy ran back down the hill into town.

There he saw a big crowd of people.

"Good morning, young man," said one of the villagers. "You're up very early this morning. And you have been running. Are you all right?"

"Yes, yes, I am. But my sheep are in danger," cried the Shepherd Boy.

"What has happened?" asked the villager. He was very concerned.

"Well, I took them to a grassy hill on the mountainside, like I do every morning. But this morning I saw a big brown wolf," the boy said.

"A WOLF?" shouted the villager.

He shouted so loudly that others came running.

"Where? Where?" shouted a woman.

And soon a bigger crowd began gathering.

"Up there with my sheep," the Shepherd Boy cried. "I'm afraid it will hurt them!"

With that, the villagers picked up their shovels and brooms. They began to run up the mountainside.

"We'll chase him away from your sheep, my lad," said the first villager. "Don't you worry."

But once they reached the top of the hillside, they found the sheep grazing quietly and happily. And there was no wolf in sight.

"Where did it go?" asked one old man.

"He must have heard you coming and decided to run down the other side of the mountain into the forest," said the Shepherd Boy.

"Well, let us know if you see it again," said the old man. And he and the rest of the villagers turned to walk down the mountain and back into town.

The young Shepherd Boy was so pleased he had made some new friends that he wasn't lonely anymore.

That is, not until a few days later.

Early one morning the Shepherd Boy drove his flock up the mountain to a new plot of grass, not far from the other.

He counted his sheep, sat down under a tree, and watched them begin to eat. It was so quiet on the hilly mountain on this sunshiny morning.

And once again the Shepherd Boy began to feel lonely.

So he jumped up and ran down the hill. He ran into the town where he saw a big crowd of villagers.

"Wolf! Wolf!" he cried. "I saw a big wolf!"

"Where? Where?" shouted the villagers.

This time the young boy's call for help drew even more people.

"It's up there with my sheep," cried the Shepherd Boy. "I'm afraid it will eat them up!"

Once again the villagers grabbed their shovels and brooms. They ran up the mountain. They were hoping to chase the big brown wolf away.

But once again when they reached the top of the hillside, there was no wolf in sight.

"Where did it go?" asked an old woman.

"I am not sure," said the boy. "He must have heard you coming and decided to run down the other side of the mountain into the forest."

Suddenly a wise-looking old man stepped out of the crowd.

"I do not believe you," he said to the Shepherd Boy. "I have looked all around on the ground. And I see no wolf tracks here or anywhere."

One by one the crowd began to look down at the ground too.

"Yes, yes, you're right," said the old woman, wagging her finger at the Shepherd Boy. "We were ready to help. But there is no wolf here. We will never believe you again!"

And with that, the villagers began walking away.

The Shepherd Boy knew he had done wrong.

"I didn't mean to hurt anyone," he said. "Please believe me. I was just so lonely. And I wanted something else to do, someone else to talk to."

But it was too late.

The crowd had disappeared.

A few mornings later, the Shepherd Boy gathered his flock of sheep around him. Once again, he walked them up to a fresh plot of green grass on the hilly mountain.

Finding a shady spot under a tree, he sat down to wait until they were finished.

All of a sudden he heard a cry!

"BAAA-aaaaah!"

The Shepherd Boy jumped up!

There, in the middle of his flock, was a big brown wolf!

"Go! Go! Leave my flock alone," shouted the Shepherd Boy.

But the wolf paid no attention to him. He was looking for something to eat for dinner!

Knowing that, the Shepherd Boy grabbed his staff and ran down the hill into town. He cried, "Wolf! Wolf! There's a big wolf on the mountain."

But this time the villagers paid no attention to him.

The poor Shepherd Boy began to cry.

"You fooled us once. Then you fooled us again. But you won't fool us a third time," said the wise old man, shaking his finger at the boy.

"It's true! It's true!" the boy cried. "Please come and see for yourself! The wolf is there!"

But no one listened to the Shepherd Boy this time.

"Once you tell a lie, no one will ever believe you again," said the wise old man. "Even when you tell the truth."

- A liar will not be believed, even when he tells the truth.

ANDROCLES

Once upon a time in a small kingdom far, far away, there lived a young boy named Androcles.

Androcles was a slave. He was owned by a very rich man called a Master. That meant Androcles had to do what he was told to do every day.

And so he did.

Each morning before anyone else was awake, Androcles would get up and fix breakfast for his Master. After that, he would feed all the animals in the barn and clean the house. Next he would do whatever else his Master ordered him to do.

And there was always something more to do.

"Sweep the floor, you lazy boy," the Master would say. "Make my dinner. And make it quick. Here, mend this shirt for me. And do it neatly."

Androcles was very sad.

One morning the Master walked by the kitchen. Androcles had just finished sweeping the floor.

"I have swept very well, sir," he said softly. "There is not a bit of dust to be found. Now your kitchen is nice and clean again for you."

"What? You call that clean?" the Master shouted. "Sweep it again, slave."

Young Androcles did as he was told. Although there was really nothing left to sweep. And once he had finished, he called to his Master once again.

"Now come and look, sir," Androcles said with a smile. "See how it shines!"

"Shines? I see no shine to the stones, slave," said the Master. "Go fetch a bucket of water from the well. Then get down on your hands and knees and scrub this floor!"

Androcles looked down.

"And don't dilly-dally," shouted the Master in a loud voice. "Be quick about it."

And so it went, day after day.

Androcles worked very hard. But no matter how hard he worked, it seemed that he could never please his Master.

One evening Androcles had an idea.

He took a piece of cloth from the cupboard. He placed a few of his belongings into it and tied the bundle to the end of a long stick. As soon as it was dark, he picked up his parcel. Androcles crept quietly out the front door and left the house of his Master.

Androcles had no money and no place to go. He just knew he had to leave there.

And so he fled to the forest to hide.

It was dark in the woods. And Androcles walked slowly and quietly because he was afraid. He was not sure what he would find there. He had heard many stories about the animals in the forest.

So when Androcles first heard the moaning and groaning, he started to turn away. Then he became curious.

He tiptoed toward the sound. He tried to avoid stepping on any branches that might crackle under his feet and make a noise.

Peeking from behind a tree, he saw a big, old Lion lying on the ground.

A shiver went up and down Androcles's back. He started to turn away.

But just then he saw that one of the Lion's paws was swollen and bleeding. He realized that the Lion could not chase him. Not with a paw that looked as sore as that one did.

So Androcles crept a little closer.

"What happened, Mister Lion?" he asked.

The Lion held up his swollen paw, and Androcles saw a huge thorn in it. That was causing all the pain.

"No wonder you are moaning and groaning, my dear Lion friend," said Androcles. "Here, let me see if I can help you."

Androcles went to the Lion and sat down beside him.

The Lion looked Androcles over very carefully before extending his paw.

"Now, don't you bite me," said Androcles. Although he was sure the Lion wouldn't do that.

Androcles took the Lion's big paw in his own two hands and tugged at the nasty thorn. Finally on the third tug, he pulled it out.

The Lion roared with pain. But he didn't bite Androcles.

In fact, when it was all over, he bent down and licked Androcles's hand. Then he limped away into the forest.

Now it was way past Androcles's bedtime, and he was very tired. So he decided to sit under a tree and rest a while before moving on. A few minutes later, the Lion came back.

"What's the matter?" asked Androcles. "Is everything all right?"

With one swoop of his big paw, the Lion picked Androcles up, placed him on his back, and carried the young boy to his cave.

Now Androcles had no time to worry. He was so tired he fell fast asleep.

The next morning when Androcles awoke, the Lion was nowhere in sight. On the ground lay some wild berries. That evening when the Lion returned, he brought home some greens and meat.

Androcles was no longer afraid of the Lion. He knew now that the Lion was trying to return a favor.

It wasn't long before the Lion and the young boy became good friends. They splashed in the river at dawn. They took long walks in the woods together. And sometimes they played hide-and-seek in the forest.

And every day, the Lion brought home berries, greens, and meat for both of them to eat.

One morning while the Lion was out hunting, Androcles decided to take a long walk in the woods by himself. But after a few hours, he was lost. As he turned to go down a path that he thought would lead him back to the Lion's lair, he ran into two soldiers.

"We have been looking for you, slave," said one of them. "We know who you are. You ran away from your Master. Now you must be punished."

"Oh, please, please, don't send me back to the Master," Androcles cried. "He was so mean to me."

"You don't understand," said the second soldier. "You are a slave, and you belong to him. You have no choice in this matter."

And with that, the two soldiers marched Androcles through the woods to the Emperor's castle where he was placed in a little room. His hands and feet were bound by heavy chains.

Androcles was so sad.

He wished he could go back to the kindly Lion who had taken such good care of him. He missed his friend.

A few days later as he was sitting there in the room, he heard someone coming down the long hall.

It was the soldiers.

The door opened, and they marched in.

"The Emperor has finally decided your punishment, runaway slave," said one of the soldiers.

"We have caught a big Lion. He has not eaten for several days. You will become his dinner tomorrow," said the other soldier.

"But, but why?" Androcles asked.

The two soldiers did not answer. They just patted him on the head and walked away laughing.

The next morning the Emperor and everyone in his court gathered in the center of the village.

Just before noon, the two soldiers came to the tiny room. They took Androcles to the big arena. Everyone stood waiting.

The big Lion stood behind steel doors.

"Ready, get set, and let him go!" shouted the Emperor.

With that the soldiers raised the big gate. And the Lion came rushing and roaring toward Androcles.

The crowd began to cheer.

Androcles closed his eyes tight. He was so afraid!

But suddenly all the noise stopped. Everyone grew very quiet. Androcles opened one eye.

Just at that moment, he felt something wet on his face.

"Go ahead. Eat me up if you have to," Androcles cried.

Nothing happened.

And the crowd was silent.

All of a sudden the big Lion licked the boy's face again with his big tongue. Much like a friendly dog.

Androcles opened both eyes.

Could it be? Yes, it was!

It was his friend the Lion—the Lion who had had a thorn in his paw.

"What is going on here?" shouted the Emperor. "I know that Lion is hungry. He has not eaten for several days."

He turned to face the cheering crowd. They were cheering again—but this time for Androcles!

The young boy had his arms around the Lion's neck and was hugging him!

"You, soldiers, bring that boy to me at once," the Emperor ordered.

They did as they were told. And Androcles sat down and told the Emperor the whole story about why he ran away. Then he told him how he had pulled the thorn from the Lion's paw.

"What a kind thing to do for an animal. I cannot hold you as a slave any longer," the Emperor told Androcles. "Nor your friend, the Lion. You have taught us a valuable lesson. You are both free to go."

Androcles reached out and put his arms around the Emperor's neck. He gave him a hug.

Then the Lion bent down and licked the Emperor's hand.

The Emperor smiled. He had never been hugged by a slave before—nor licked by a Lion. It felt good.

Soon the whole crowd of people began hugging one another.

It was a beautiful sight!

A few minutes later, Androcles climbed on the Lion's back and waved good-bye to the cheering crowd. Then the two friends went happily into the forest.

- Few people ever forget a kindness.

The Play

ANDROCLES

Cast of Characters
Narrator
Androcles
Master
The Lion
First Soldier
Second Soldier
The Emperor
Townsfolk

TALES OF AESOP

Act One

Narrator: Once upon a time in a tiny kingdom, far away from here, there lived a young boy named Androcles. He was a slave. He was owned by a very rich man called a Master. Each morning Androcles would rise very early and prepare breakfast for his Master. Then he would feed all the animals in the barn, clean the house, and do whatever else his Master told him to do. He worked very hard. But no matter how hard he worked, Androcles could not please his Master.

Androcles: I have finished sweeping the floor, Master. Now it is nice and clean for you once again.

Master: What? You call that clean? Sweep it again, slave!

Narrator: Young Androcles did as he was told. Although there was really nothing to sweep. Once he had finished, he called to his Master once again.

Androcles: I have swept the floor really well, sir. Now come and look! See how it shines!

Master: Shines? I see no shine to the stones, you silly slave! Go fetch a bucket of water from the well and bring it back. Then get down on your hands and knees and scrub my floor! I want it as white as the lily that grows in my garden.

Androcles: Yes, Master.

Master: And don't dilly-dally. Be quick about it!

Narrator: Once again Androcles did as he was told. And once again he called to the Master when he was done. The Master looked at the floor, stared at the young boy, and walked away saying nothing. There was nothing he could say. The floor was as clean as it could be.

Androcles knew that the same thing would just happen all over again the next morning. So that evening Androcles took a piece of cloth from the cupboard. He placed his few belongings on it and tied the bundle to the end of a long stick.

As soon as it was dark, he picked up the stick and tiptoed out the door. Then he ran as fast as his young legs would carry him—right into the forest.

Act Two

Narrator: Androcles began wandering through the woods. He was trying to find a safe place to hide. It was so dark that he didn't know which way to go. Yet each step was leading him farther into the forest. Finally he came to a thicket of bushes.

Androcles: I think I will sit down and rest a while. I know I will be safe here until morning. Then I must move again. If they find me, they may send me back to the Master.

Narrator: Androcles pulled a small blanket from his parcel. He curled up under the biggest bush and closed his eyes. Suddenly he heard a big crackling noise. Androcles opened his eyes. He jumped up and looked around.

Androcles: Oh! What's that?

Lion: Grrrrrr.

Androcles: That sounds like a Lion!

Narrator: Androcles looked long and hard. But he could see nothing in the darkness.

Lion: GRRRRRRR!

Narrator: The sound was louder and closer than before! Androcles huddled closer to the bush. Then just at that moment the moon began to rise over the mountain. Its light cast a soft glow through the tops of the trees. There on the ground lay a big Lion, moaning and groaning. Oh, he's big, thought Androcles, as he turned to run away. But looking back once more, he saw that the Lion was not moving. In the dim light, he looked injured.

Androcles: Dear friend Lion, are you all right?

Lion: Grrrrr. No, you silly boy! Can't you see I'm not all right? I have been hurt badly.

Narrator: Androcles crept a little closer. Now he could see that one of the Lion's paws was swollen and bleeding. He went and sat down beside him.

Androcles: What happened, Mister Lion?

Lion: Well, I was running through the forest, trying to find something for my dinner. All of a sudden I stepped on a tree limb and fell into a bush. It was filled with thorns. I got most of them out except this big one.

Androcles: Well, no wonder you are moaning and groaning, my dear friend. Here, let me see if I can help you. Give me your paw.

Narrator: Androcles took the Lion's big furry paw in his hands and pulled out the nasty thorn.

Lion: Aarrrrgh! That really hurt!

Androcles: I'm sorry, Mister Lion. But at least it's out now. Make your way down to the river and soak your paw in the nice cool water. I am sure it will feel much better.

Lion: That sounds like a good idea, boy. It's beginning to feel better already. Thank you for helping me.

Narrator: And with that, the big Lion bent down and licked Androcles's hand. Then he limped away. Androcles was tired. It was way past his bedtime. He looked around, found a tree, and sat down to rest. But a few minutes later, the Lion came stomping back through the forest.

Lion: Say, I was just thinking about something, my friend. Do you have a place to sleep tonight?

Androcles: Well, actually, no, I don't, Mister Lion. I am a slave, and I have run away from my Master. I came to the forest hoping he would not find me here. He might even forget about me.

Lion: Then it's settled.

Androcles: What's settled?

Lion: You must come and stay with me. I have plenty of room in my cave, and I will take good care of you. Just as you have taken good care of me.

Narrator: The Lion then picked up the young boy. He placed him on his back and carried him to his cave.

Act Three

Narrator: The next morning when Androcles awoke, the Lion was nowhere in sight. But on the ground beside him lay some wild berries. That evening when the Lion returned, he brought the young slave some meat and greens. This act was repeated each day. And soon Androcles and the Lion became fast friends, happily spending time together. Each morning they splashed in the river. Then they took a long walk in the woods and picked berries. Sometimes they played hide-and-seek around the trees. But one morning when Androcles awoke, he found that the Lion was not feeling too well.

Androcles: You just lie and rest. I will go out alone and see what I can find for our breakfast and dinner.

Lion: All right. But don't go too far. Yesterday some of the other animals said they spotted some men in the forest.

Androcles: All right. I will be home before sundown, my friend.

Narrator: Androcles went on his way, stopping to play in the river as he and the Lion did each morning. Then he picked some greens, stopped to eat a few berries, and watched some rabbits play tag. The sun was shining, and the birds were singing. Singing so loud, in fact, that Androcles never heard the voices behind him. All of a sudden a hand reached out and grabbed Androcles's shoulder.

First Soldier: Say, what do you think you're doing, boy?

Androcles: Uh, uh, nothing, sir. I mean, I didn't hear you coming. Uh, I mean, nothing, nothing . . .

Second Soldier: Nothing? What kind of an answer is that? Nothing? Did you know that this forest belongs to the Emperor?

First Soldier: Yes, and did you know that no one walks in this forest without the Emperor's permission?

Androcles: No, I didn't know that, sir. Uh, sirs.

Second Soldier: Say, you look kind of familiar. I heard that a slave boy ran away from his Master several weeks ago. Might you be that slave?

Narrator: Androcles looked down at the ground. And with that, one of the soldiers pulled a steel chain from his pocket and chained Androcles's wrists together.

First Soldier: We have been looking for you, slave. You ran away from your Master. Now you must be punished.

Androcles: Please, please don't make me go back to the Master. He was so mean to me.

Second Soldier: You belong to him. You are a slave. You have no choice in this matter.

Narrator: As Androcles began to cry, the two soldiers marched him through the woods toward the Emperor's castle.

Act Four

Narrator: Upon reaching the Emperor's castle, Androcles was taken to a little room where his hands and feet were bound with heavy chains. He was so sad. He missed his good friend, the kindly Lion, who had taken such good care of him. Several days later, Androcles heard someone coming down the long hallway toward his room. The door opened. There stood the soldiers.

First Soldier: So how does it feel to be back home?

Second Soldier: Look how he sits there with such a sad look on his face. You should have thought about what might happen before you decided to run away, boy.

First Soldier: Well, never fear. The Emperor has decided on a good punishment for you.

Second Soldier: Yes, he has. Last evening we caught a big Lion that has not eaten for several days. He is so hungry, poor thing. You will be his dinner. What do you think of that?

Narrator: The two soldiers patted poor Androcles on the head. They opened the door to the little room and walked away laughing.

Act Five

Narrator: Early the next morning, the Emperor's soldiers began posting notices in the village. The notices told of a big show. And all were invited. Just before noon the two soldiers went to the little room. They took Androcles to the big arena where all the townsfolk stood watching and waiting. When everyone was there, the Emperor made his announcement.

Emperor: We have here a young runaway slave, my people. Since he left, his Master has been so hungry. And his house, so dirty. That was not a kind thing to do to the poor Master. We must teach this young boy a lesson about kindness.

Narrator: Androcles stared at the ground. The chains had been taken from his arms and legs. But where could he run to get away? The townsfolk began to cheer. When they saw the big Lion standing behind some steel doors, their shouts became louder.

First Soldier: We are ready, your highness.

Second Soldier: The Lion is very hungry, your highness.

Emperor: All right then. Ready. Set. Let him go.

Narrator: The big gate was raised. And the Lion began to roar as he rushed toward Androcles. The young boy closed his eyes tightly. The townsfolk cheered. Then all of a sudden everything was quiet. Androcles stood very still. He opened one eye. Just at that moment, he felt something wet on his face.

Androcles: Go ahead. Eat me up if you have to.

Narrator: The big Lion licked Androcles's face with his tongue like a friendly dog. Androcles opened both eyes and stared at the Lion. Could it be? Yes, it was! It was his friend, the Lion. The Lion who had had a thorn in his paw. Androcles threw his arms around the Lion's neck and hugged him.

Emperor: What is going on here? What is the meaning of this? I know that this Lion is hungry. He has not eaten for several days.

First Soldier: Why, we don't know, your highness.

Second Soldier: Something is definitely wrong here.

Emperor: All right, you soldiers. I order you to bring that boy to me at once. I want to know the meaning of this!

Narrator: The soldiers did as they were told. Androcles sat down and told the Emperor the whole story. He went clear back to the way he had been treated by his Master. And why he had run away. Then he told him about the day he had pulled the thorn from the Lion's paw and how they became fast friends.

Emperor: What a kind thing to do for an animal. You have taught all of us a valuable lesson about kindness, my boy. I cannot hold you as a slave any longer. Nor your friend, the Lion. You are both free to go.

Narrator: The crowd cheered once again. Androcles reached out, put his arms around the Emperor's neck, and gave him a hug. Then the Lion bent down and licked the Emperor's hand. The Emperor smiled. He had never been hugged by a slave before nor licked by a Lion. It felt good. A few minutes later Androcles climbed up on the Lion's back and waved good-bye to the cheering crowd. Then the two friends went happily into the forest.

- Few people ever forget a kindness.